TWO-FACE'S DOUBLE TAKE

WRITTEN BY
MATTHEW K. MANNING

ILLUSTRATED BY
**SHAWN McMANUS AND
LEE LOUGHRIDGE**

BATMAN CREATED BY
BOB KANE

Raintree

08 APR 2015

Visit our website to find out
more information about
Raintree books.

Fax +44 (0) 1865 312263
Email myorders@raintreepublishers.co.uk

Customers from outside the UK please telephone +44 1865 312262

Raintree is an imprint of Capstone Global Library Limited,
a company incorporated in England and Wales having its registered office
at 7 Pilgrim Street, London, EC4V 6LB – Registered company number: 6695582

First published by Stone Arch Books in 2010
First published in the United Kingdom in hardback and paperback in 2010
The moral rights of the proprietor have been asserted.

Art Director: Bob Lentz
Designer: Brann Garvey
Production Specialist: Michelle Biedschied
Editor: Vaarunika Dharmapala
Originated by Capstone Global Library Ltd
Printed and bound in China by Leo Paper Products Ltd

ISBN 978 1 406217 95 7 (hardback)
14 13 12 11 10
10 9 8 7 6 5 4 3 2 1

ISBN 978 1 406218 03 9 (paperback)
14 13
10 9 8 7 6 5 4 3

British Library Cataloguing in Publication Data
A full catalogue record for this book is available from the British Library.

CONTENTS

CHAPTER 1

TWO BIRDS

It was quiet outside the Second National Bank in central Gotham City. Most of the local business people had gone home after a long day at work. Scraps of paper blew across the otherwise empty street. It was a dull summer evening.

BARROOOOMM!!

Suddenly, the doors of the bank shot off their hinges. They crashed down on to the pavement. Smoke spilled out of the entrance into the purple evening sky.

Two figures appeared in the doorway. They walked casually down the bank's granite steps and past a lamp post. As the bank's alarm rang in the air, the smoke began to clear. In the light stood the red-headed Poison Ivy and her villainess partner, Harley Quinn.

"Not a bad haul, Red," Harley said. She followed Ivy to their pink convertible which was parked across the street. Each woman had a duffel bag full of money over her shoulder. "I could get used to this."

"Well, don't," Poison Ivy said. She threw her bag on to the back seat of the car. Several other bags were already piled inside. "We're just repaying a debt to an old friend. After tonight, we'll go back to business as usual."

"You're the boss," Harley said.

Harley jumped into the passenger seat. She unzipped her bag and pulled out a wad of bank notes. "But you've got to love the fringe benefits," Harley said.

Ivy looked over at Harley and smiled. Harley was quite the spectacle in that jester's suit of hers. No matter how hard Poison Ivy tried to stay serious, she couldn't help but return her partner's grin. Harley was certainly crazy, but she never failed to make Poison Ivy laugh.

Suddenly, Harley's expression changed to one of pure surprise. Ivy looked over at Harley's hand. It was still clutching the wad of stolen bank notes, but now, there was a thin black cord wrapped around her arm.

"Wha – ?" Harley started to say. Then suddenly, something yanked her out of the car. WHOOOOSH!

Poison Ivy looked up. Harley was dangling from the lamp post overhead. "A little help, please!" Harley called down.

Ivy wasn't listening. It was time to make her getaway. Harley was good for a laugh, but stopping to help her wasn't worth getting sent back to prison.

Ivy jammed her key into the ignition. As she was about to turn it, a Batarang struck the back of her hand. **THWACK!** She turned around in the driver's seat. She couldn't see who had thrown the weapon, but she knew he was there, somewhere.

THUD! Poison Ivy spun back towards the front of her car and screamed.

Batman had found her. The Dark Knight crouched on the bonnet of her car, his black cape draped across the windscreen.

Ivy quickly reached over and opened the glove compartment. As Batman lunged forwards to stop her, she pulled out her trusty wrist crossbow. Before she could shoot, Batman reached inside the car and grabbed her arm.

Poison Ivy thrashed wildly, but Batman was unfazed. "That's enough, Ivy," he said. "Your little crime spree is over."

High above Ivy's head, Harley was also struggling. The Batrope was tight around Harley's wrist. With her free hand, she reached into her boot and pulled out a small glass vial.

CRUNCH! Harley smashed the vial against the cord. A bright green liquid poured out. **FZZT!** Quickly, the chemical began to eat through the rope. Harley could feel it weakening.

Harley glanced down at the street below her. "Perhaps I should've thought this through a little more," she said to herself.

Meanwhile, Batman was reaching into his Utility Belt. He removed a pair of black, bat-shaped handcuffs and attached one to Ivy's wrist. "Robbing banks isn't like you," Batman said. "What's going on, Isley?"

"Don't you dare call me that!" Ivy said. "Pamela Isley died years ago. I'm Pois –"

WHAM! Harley Quinn fell, landing right on top of Batman. Taken by surprise, Batman fell off the bonnet of the car. **THUD!** He hit the street hard, cushioning Harley's fall.

"Hiya, Red!" Harley said, landing on top of Batman. "Mind if I drop –"

"Don't say it," Ivy interrupted.

Poison Ivy turned the key in the ignition. "Just get back in the car, Harley," she said.

"Okey-dokey," Harley said, leaping into the passenger seat.

Batman shook his head and quickly got to his feet. He was too late. Harley and Ivy were already speeding down the street. They were well out of his reach now.

Batman smiled. He knew where they were going next. After all, this was the fourth bank the two had robbed tonight. Batman had worked out their pattern.

He pressed a button on his Utility Belt. In an instant, the Batmobile pulled up beside him. The cockpit opened by itself, and Batman jumped into the driver's seat. As he slammed down on the pedal, the dashboard TV console turned on. **CLICK!**

A familiar face appeared on the screen. It was Alfred – the longtime butler of Batman's other identity, Bruce Wayne.

"I was wondering where you were, sir," Alfred said.

"No time to chat, Alfred," Batman said. "I need to catch up to Harley."

"It'll have to wait, I'm afraid," Alfred interrupted. "Or did you forget that you have other plans this evening?"

Batman sighed. He had completely forgotten. "The charity ball," he said.

"Indeed, Master Bruce," Alfred said. "One would think that the Children's Hospital is just as worthy a cause as swapping punches with any villain."

Batman knew Alfred was right. Bruce Wayne had responsibilities, too.

Batman grunted. It often felt like he was living two lives. It was difficult to balance his responsibilities as Batman with his responsibilities as Bruce Wayne.

SKREEE-EEE-EEECH!

The Batmobile's tyres squealed as Batman quickly spun the car around. "I'll be right there, Alfred," Batman said, switching off the monitor. Then he tapped another button on the Batmobile's dashboard. "Right after I make a quick call," he said to himself.

CHAPTER 2

SPLIT DECISION

Jon Roscetti hadn't been working at his new job for long. So, when he heard his boss arguing with someone in the bedroom, he decided to check up on him. After all, one of his duties was to make sure the boss was always safe. Jon crept down the dimly lit corridor of the luxury flat. The two voices grew louder.

". . . Two of everything, that's what we need," said the first voice. The man sounded calm, and Jon instantly recognized the voice of his boss.

"It's not enough," said the second voice in an angry growl. "Think about it. Yeah, we've got all the obvious things. Two cars, two houses, all of that. But it's not about possessions. They won't help us beat the Batman."

"I don't understand," said Jon's boss.

Jon crept closer. He saw a shadowy figure in the dark bedroom, but he couldn't see who his boss was arguing with.

"No, you obviously *don't* understand," said the harsh voice. "And that's why we're not complete!"

"Complete?" asked Jon's boss.

"There's only one of us!" said the angry voice. "It doesn't work. We can't win without a partner."

A bolt of lightning illuminated the room. "Hm," Jon's boss said, momentarily bathed in light. "A partner?"

Jon's boss used to be a good-looking man. In fact, the newspapers had called him "Handsome Harvey". That was years ago – before the accident.

"That's right," the voice said. "A partner. There has to be two. Another one just like us."

"So, the real question is 'who?'" Jon's boss said.

"That's right," said the angry voice. "Who is like us? Who has fortune, fame, and the perfect life? Who can we bring down to our level?"

As Jon continued to peek into the room, he accidentally pushed the door forwards.

The door swayed on its hinges and let out a soft creak. Jon's boss turned around and looked at him. Now his full face could be seen in the moonlight. Half of it was still handsome, but the other half was scarred and greenish blue. It made perfect sense that after his accident, Harvey Dent had renamed himself Two-Face.

"Get out of here!" Two-Face growled.

Jon turned and ran down the corridor in a panic. He would never get used to the way his new boss looked. His face was like something out of a horror film.

"As we were saying," Two-Face said to himself. "Who is Gotham's favourite son? Who do we make just like us?"

Two-Face smiled. He answered himself in a calm voice, "It's obvious. Bruce Wayne."

Two-Face took a special coin out of his pocket. He always left important decisions up to chance – heads or tails, yes or no. He flipped the coin into the air and snatched it quickly with the other hand. When he slapped it down on the back of his hand, the weird coin's scarred side was facing up.

Two-Face's lips curled into a sinister smile. *Soon,* he thought to himself, *Bruce Wayne will come face to face with a side of himself that he's never seen!*

CHAPTER 3

TWO FOR THE ROAD

"Brucie! It's so good of you to finally show up," said Veronica Vreeland.

Bruce handed his coat to one of the waiters at the charity ball. "You know me, Veronica," Bruce said with a sly smile. "Always making a dramatic entrance."

Veronica produced a rather fake laugh. She patted Bruce's lapel. "Of course," she said. "I should have known."

"Can I get you something to drink, sir?" asked a voice behind Bruce.

Bruce turned to see a skinny young man with light hair and a nervous smile.

"Just water for now, thanks," Bruce answered, smiling at the young waiter.

Veronica took Bruce's arm and walked him into the hospital. The normally bare hospital walls had been decorated for the evening with large, dramatic curtains. They gave the event a feeling of glitz and glamour. It was exactly the type of party Gotham's rich and famous were used to attending.

Bruce glanced at Veronica as they walked. He had known her for years. They both came from wealthy Gotham City families. While Veronica loved the spotlight, Bruce was more comfortable in the shadows.

"It was so good of you to organize this event," Veronica said, smiling up at her handsome date.

"It was nothing, really," Bruce said. "My butler did most of the work."

Veronica laughed her fake laugh once again. Bruce smiled at her, but his thoughts were straying. He shouldn't have let Poison Ivy get away. He should have kept an eye on Harley Quinn. His mind felt divided between where he was, and where he should be. Hopefully, the message he had left earlier would reach his partners.

"Are you okay?" Veronica asked. "You seem to be a million miles away."

"I'm fine," Bruce said, clearing his throat. "Just thirsty." Bruce raised a finger in the air as the waiter walked by him.

"How's that water coming along?" he asked the awkward waiter.

"Sir?" the waiter asked, confused.

"I ordered a water from you," Bruce said.

"No, sir, you didn't order anything from me," the waiter said.

Just then, Bruce noticed someone out of the corner of his eye. It was a young man who looked exactly like the waiter he was talking to. "Oh," Bruce said as the second man brought him his water. "My mistake."

Bruce turned back to Veronica. For the first time that night, she was laughing a genuine laugh.

"Twins," she said, smiling widely.

Bruce looked around the room. There were eight waiters in total.

All eight waiters were dressed in vests and bow ties and seemed a bit nervous. The strange thing was that each waiter had an identical twin working beside him.

That's odd, Bruce thought. *Four sets of twins in the same place?* Suddenly, Bruce realized what was going on. He knew what he had to do.

"Excuse me for a moment, will you?" Bruce asked Veronica. "I need to get a little fresh air."

Veronica let out a fake laugh again as Bruce hurried away. His walk turned into a jog as he neared a doorway to the stairs. The stairwell was empty and just shadowy enough so that he wouldn't be seen.

Bruce began to unbutton his shirt, revealing his Batman uniform underneath.

RAT-TAT-TAT! RAT-TAT-TAT!

It was too late. He could hear weapons firing inside the ballroom.

Peering through the small window on the door, Bruce realized his suspicion had been correct. Waltzing into the room was none other than Two-Face.

"Hands up!" Two-Face yelled. "Both of them!"

Bruce watched as the rich men and women raised their hands. Every single one of them looked terrified.

"Here's the deal," Two-Face said. "We don't want your cash, and we couldn't care less about your jewels. We came here for one reason."

Bruce pressed his ear against the door in order to hear better.

"We want Bruce Wayne!" Two-Face screamed. "Give him to us, and we'll leave the rest of you alone! And if you don't . . ."

Bruce looked down at the bat-symbol on his chest. He could rush into the ballroom as Batman, but that would put countless lives in danger. He really had no choice. He had to give himself up.

Bruce Wayne buttoned up his shirt and pushed open the stairwell door. "I'm right here, Harvey," he said, raising his hands.

"Get him, boys," Two-Face rumbled.

The four sets of twin waiters surrounded Bruce. Two of Two-Face's twin thugs put a cloth bag over Bruce's head. Then everything went black.

CHAPTER 4

DOUBLE TROUBLE

"Up and at 'em, Bruce," Two-Face said as he pulled the bag off of Bruce Wayne's head. "Nap time's over."

Bruce looked around. He was standing on the second-floor catwalk of what looked like a chemical plant. The factory was poorly lit, but he could see several giant vats of boiling liquid below. Hisssssss

Bruce tried to move his arms, but both hands were tied behind his back. In front of him stood Two-Face's eight henchmen. All of them were armed.

"What's the meaning of this, Harvey?" Bruce asked angrily.

"Now, now," Two-Face said, patting Bruce on the back. "Is that any way to talk to an old friend?"

"You're not the man I used to know," Bruce said.

"That's true," Two-Face began. "But after tonight, *you* won't be the man you used to know, either."

"What are you saying?" Bruce asked, narrowing his eyes.

Harvey turned his good side towards Bruce. "We're old pals, Brucie," Harvey said. "We go way back. Years ago you were even going to be my best man when I was about to marry Pamela Isley."

"Harvey –" Bruce tried to speak.

"You were like me," Two-Face interrupted. "A real hero to the people."

Two-Face turned away from Bruce, so that only his scarred side was visible. "Well, now you're going to be like me once again, Bruce!" Two-Face said harshly. "I'll bring out your inner menace."

A pair of Two-Face's henchmen walked over to Bruce and led him forward. Bruce moved slowly along the narrow catwalk until he was right above one of the bubbling vats.

"You'll be my partner, old friend," Two-Face said. "But first, you need a little makeover – something to bring out your dark side."

"Stay put, Wayne," said Jon Roscetti, one of Two-Face's henchmen.

Bruce recognized the man as the waiter he had ordered a drink from at the ball. Jon kept his weapon trained on Bruce as both he and his twin brother slowly backed away to join the rest of Two-Face's men.

Harvey and his men were standing above another vat of chemicals, but their eyes were fixed on the vat right below Bruce. "Do you know where we are?" Two-Face asked Bruce. "This is the place that made me. An explosion here gave me my new look."

Two-Face paused, pointing to his scarred face. "I'm going to do the same to you, old friend," he said. "That vat down there is rigged to blow at the touch of a button."

"Don't do this, Harvey," Bruce said. He began to struggle, but his hands were tightly bound.

"Don't worry," Two-Face said. "We're doing this for your own good." Two-Face reached into his pocket and removed a remote control.

"You're not thinking straight," Bruce said. He reached under his suit jacket and into his Utility Belt. His fingers closed over a small capsule.

"This isn't going to kill you," Two-Face said, ignoring Bruce. He raised his remote into the air. "It'll just make you stronger!"

Just as Two-Face was about to trigger the remote, Bruce turned and tossed the capsule. It landed in the vat directly below Two-Face and his men. The capsule contained a small plastic explosive.

The entire catwalk shook as the vat erupted like a volcano. Two-Face and his men dived to the side to avoid the blast. Several henchmen grabbed on to the railing for support.

Concealed by smoke and flames, Bruce reached into his Utility Belt for a knife. He quickly cut himself free from the rope. He began to run down the catwalk, away from Two-Face's men.

"Get him!" Two-Face yelled. A thick pillar of black smoke had covered the entire catwalk and his men couldn't see anything. They fired their weapons blindly into the fog.

Suddenly, Jon saw a shadowy figure walking towards him. "There he is!" he yelled. "There's Wayne!"

The figure stepped out of the smoke and smiled. "Not quite," he said. Two-Face's men all took a big step backwards.

Standing only a few metres away from them was Batman. Suddenly, a shadowy, black-gloved fist sliced through the smoke-filled air.

CHAPTER 5

TWO FOR ONE

RAT·TAT·TAT!

The sound of weapons firing echoed inside the factory. The smoke was still too thick to see through. None of Two-Face's men could spot their target.

SMASH! Gloved black hands shot out of the smoke, knocking one of Two-Face's thugs against the wall behind him.

SLAM! A black boot sent a swift kick to another henchman's stomach. Batman was moving through the fog unseen. He truly was a creature of the darkness.

Two-Face watched worriedly as the Dark Knight attacked several of his men. Then, he backed away from the catwalk and headed towards the spiral metal staircase.

Meanwhile, Batman was lifting a man into the air. He effortlessly tossed him towards his twin brother across the platform.

CLINK CLANK! Batarangs shot out and struck two more of Two-Face's men. Batman did a quick count in his head. Seven of Two-Face's men were down. Only one remained.

Batman heard footsteps pounding against metal. He saw Jon Roscetti sprinting blindly across the catwalk. The young crook turned to see if Batman was following him.

In his panic, Roscetti ran smack into a support beam. **Oomf!** Jon slumped to the ground. Batman shrugged. "That was easy," he said to himself.

Another vat exploded, sending boiling orange chemicals into the air. Two-Face had triggered the bomb he'd intended for Bruce Wayne. Batman raised his cape and crouched beneath it. The chemicals splashed off its fire-resistant material. Two-Face had used up his trump card.

Outside, Two-Face was running across the factory's empty car park. Suddenly, he felt a thin cord wrap around his legs. He fell, dropping his weapon on the hard ground. **KRAK!** As he struggled to free himself, he glanced upwards. Standing over him was Batman.

The Dark Knight's cape was blowing in the gentle evening breeze. Batman's hands held the other end of the Batrope.

"It's over, Two-Face," he said.

Two-Face started laughing. "I would have thought you'd know me better by now, Bats," he said. As Batman pulled Two-Face to his feet, the Batmobile pulled up behind them. Two-Face continued, "I always have two plans up my sleeve. In a matter of minutes, I'll have enough money to buy my way out of any crimes the cops charge me with."

"Not this time!" came a voice from inside the Batmobile. The top slid open and Robin leaped out of the cockpit, looking at Two-Face. "This jailbird won't be flying free any time soon."

"Those puns stopped being funny about two years ago," said Batgirl as she stood up in the driver's seat.

"You got my message," Batman said to his two partners. He leaned Two-Face up against the side of the car. Batman placed his handcuffs around Two-Face's wrists.

"Yup," Robin said. "And it was just like you said. Harley and Ivy tried to hit the Second Avenue LexBank. We were waiting for them."

"Not to say they didn't go down without a fight," Batgirl added. She picked a thorn out of her hair and flicked it to the ground. "But Two-Face won't be buying his way out of this one!" Batgirl said, smiling.

Two-Face's confident smile quickly disappeared. "You knew . . ." he mumbled.

"I worked out what you were up to hours ago," Batman said. "After I heard Ivy mention something about repaying old debts. That's why you had your engagement to Pamela Isley on your mind earlier."

Two-Face was speechless.

"Poison Ivy broke your heart before you became Two-Face," Batman continued. "So she agreed to run a few errands for you now that you're in the same line of work. She thought she owed you a favour. I bet you even suggested that she should work with a partner."

Police sirens sounded in the distance as Batman continued to talk, "Your patterns are too predictable, Harvey. Banks that are connected to the number '2'. A pair of criminals. Two crimes at once."

"Hmph," Two-Face grunted. He looked over at Batgirl and Robin. The sirens of the police cars grew louder. "That's something else we have in common, Bats," he said. "We both understand the need for partners."

Three police cars pulled into the factory car park. Two-Face stared at the flashing lights and then stood up straight. He looked Batman in the eye. "I guess we're more alike than I had thought," he said.

Batman reached into his Utility Belt and pulled out his grapnel gun. He shot it into the air towards a neighbouring building.

As Batman soared upwards to the building, Batgirl and Robin settled back into the seats of the Batmobile. They revved the engine and prepared to follow their boss.

The police cars pulled up next to Two-Face, surrounding him with the wail of their sirens. Two-Face didn't notice them. His eyes were fixed on his old friend – who was now his enemy.

The cool evening air enveloped Batman as he swung on his line. Soaring quickly up to the nearby building's rooftop, Batman landed gracefully. He paused for a second and looked back down at his former friend.

"We're more alike than you'll ever know, Harvey," Batman said under his breath. With that, Batman – and Bruce Wayne – disappeared into the night.

Two-Face

REAL NAME: Harvey Dent

OCCUPATION: Professional criminal

BASE: Gotham City

HEIGHT:
1 m 83 cm

WEIGHT:
82 kg

EYES:
Blue

HAIR:
Brown/grey

Once considered Gotham's "White Knight," Harvey Dent waged his war on crime the traditional way – through the court system. He developed a reputation as the best lawyer in the country and jailed many of Gotham's most dangerous criminals. Harvey had a temper, but he could usually control it – until an accident disfigured half of his face. Then his darker side took control. As Two-Face, Harvey has become a man of two minds, with each side constantly at war with the other.

G.C.P.D. GOTHAM CITY POLICE DEPARTMENT

- Two-Face is divided between good and evil, and either side can take control at any time. When it comes to a difficult decision, he resorts to flipping his lucky coin to choose his course of action.

- Harvey has an obsession with twos because of his double personality. His crimes often involve pairs or twins, and he always has a back-up plan in case one scheme fails.

- Before the explosion changed Harvey Dent into Two-Face, Bruce Wayne and Dent were close friends. Bruce still hopes that Harvey's good side will one day retake control and return Gotham's greatest lawyer to his original form.

- Before becoming Two-Face, Harvey had loved Pamela Isley, who is now known as Poison Ivy, the super-villainess. The two had been engaged to be married – and Bruce Wayne was going to be Harvey's best man.

CONFIDENTIAL

BIOGRAPHIES

Matthew K. Manning has taken several tours of Gotham City in his life. He's written issues of DC Comics' *The Batman Strikes!* and *Justice League Adventures*, as well as a history of the character, *The Batman Vault*. He's also spent his fair share of time in other metropolises, writing comics or books about the Legion of Super-Heroes, Looney Tunes, Spider-Man, Wolverine, and Iron Man.

Shawn McManus has been drawing pictures ever since he was able to hold a pencil in his tiny hand. Since then, he has illustrated comic books featuring Sandman, Batman, Dr. Fate, Spider-Man, and many others. Shawn has also done work for film, animation, and online entertainment.

Lee Loughridge has been working in comics for more than 14 years. He currently lives in a tent on the beach.

GLOSSARY

casually calmly

dangling hanging loosely

enveloped covered or surrounded something completely

glamour fashion, charm, or appeal

ignition electrical system that activates a device

jester joker, similar to a clown

menace threat or danger

sinister something evil and threatening

spectacle remarkable and dramatic sight

suspicion thought, based more on feeling than on fact, that something is wrong

vial small container, usually used to hold liquids

DISCUSSION QUESTIONS

1. Which character in this book was your favourite? What are your reasons?

2. This book has several sets of twins in it. Have you ever met any twins? What would be good and bad about having a twin sibling?

3. Do you think Two-Face could become a hero once again? Why or why not?

WRITING PROMPTS

1. Both Bruce Wayne and Two-Face believe they have a lot in common with each other. What kinds of things make them alike? How are they different? Write down your ideas.

2. Batman asks his friends Batgirl and Robin for help. Have you ever asked anyone for help? What was the result? Write about your partnership.

3. Batman was able to figure out Two-Face's plans using his detective skills. Have you ever solved a puzzle or problem on your own? Write about how you did it.

MORE NEW BATMAN ADVENTURES!

ROBIN'S FIRST FLIGHT

BAT-MITE'S
BIG BLUNDER

KILLER CROC HUNTER

MY FROZEN VALENTINE

THE MAN BEHIND
THE MASK